For My Family, Love, Allie

WRITTEN AND PHOTOGRAPHED BY

Ellen B. Senisi

Albert Whitman & Company • Morton Grove, Illinois

To the best young woman I know: my daughter, Kate,
with love and thanks for everything, including her work
as photographer's assistant for this book.

I would like to acknowledge the Edwards and Read families,
who allowed me to photograph them.
A special thanks to them for sharing on camera
the family love that overcomes all differences.

"They're coming tomorrow," thought Allie. "What should I do?"

Allie's relatives from out of town were coming for a big family party. They would all have fun together. They would bring gifts for Allie's family. Allie wanted to give them something back. What could it be?

Allie could do many things very well. She could do things her little sister and brother couldn't do yet.

She could read to Meagan.

She could make a sandwich for Jonathan.

But Allie wasn't grown-up. She couldn't go into a store and buy presents for people. What could she give?

Allie pushed her plate away and stretched. She looked at her hands. These hands could do many things. Could she *make* a present? Like what? Allie looked at her sticky fingers.

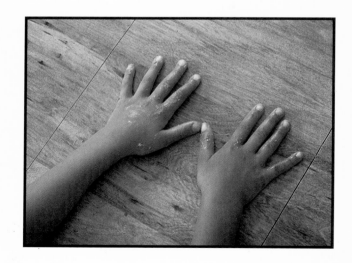

That was it! Allie ran into the kitchen.

"Mom, I want to make food to give to everyone at the party."

Allie's mom thought food was a great idea.

"But, Mom," Allie said, "is food really a present?"

"Of course," said her mother. "Homemade food is always a special gift. You know, people give each other lots of things that don't come wrapped up or aren't bought in stores."

"Good," said Allie. "Then I can eat some of whatever I make. I like that kind of present."

After lunch, Allie's Grandma Edwards came.

"What's in this big bag, Grandma?" asked Allie.

"Things we need to cook with for dinner today and the party tomorrow."

"And what's in the little bag?"

"Oh, things for you kids to play with," she said, "while your mother and I work."

"But Grandma," said Allie, "can't I help?"

"I guess you're getting old enough," Grandma Edwards said.

So Allie got to help make some Jamaican food. Her grandmother showed Allie how to peel and cut plantains.

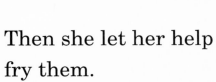

Then she let her help fry them.

Next, Allie helped make her grandma's special chicken soup. Then they made dumplings for the soup. Three sets of hands rolled dough into dumplings.

"Whew," said Allie's mom when they were done. "That was a lot of work. You can go play, Allie."

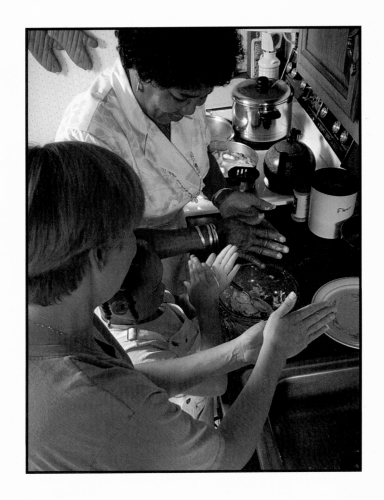

"No!" said Allie. "Now it's my turn to make my present."

"But Allie," said her mother, "you just helped us make food."

Allie slumped down to the floor. "It's not the same thing. I didn't make anything all by myself yet!"

Allie ran out of the kitchen with tears in her eyes. She ran to the wooden swing in the yard and cried. Still nothing for her to give.

After a little while, Allie's mom came outside. She had a cold drink for each of them and a book.

"This is a cookbook for kids," she said. "Let's see if there's something you could make in here."

Allie gave her mom a kiss. They looked through the book and chose a recipe called "Peanut-Butter Treats."

Allie ran back into the house to get started.
She got out the big blue bowl. She put into it:

peanut butter
powdered milk
confectioner's sugar
and raisins.
She mashed and moshed the squishy mixture.

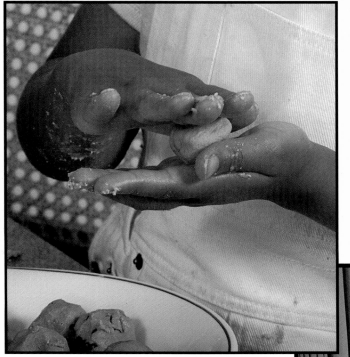

She kept going till
the mixture felt smooth.
Then she shaped lumps
of dough into balls.

It wasn't that easy.
The dough was very
sticky. And some of the
balls wouldn't get round.

But the plates slowly
began to fill up.

Allie rolled some of the balls in white coconut flakes. She rolled some in brown cocoa powder. She left some plain. What a beautiful mix of colors!

Then Allie rolled more in decorations of all colors.

"Allie," called her mother, "time to clean up!"

Allie suddenly felt very tired. But she still had to do an enormous cleanup.

"Daddy," said Allie at bedtime, "today I made treats for the party."

"Did you? I'm proud of you, pumpkin."

"They're so good, you're really going to like them."

"Great! I'll eat them up now and you can make more tomorrow for everyone else."

"Oh, Daddy!"

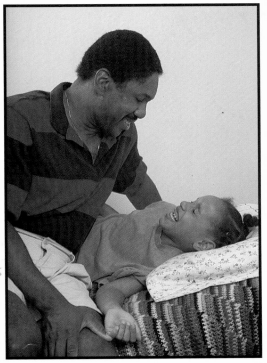

The next morning, Grandpa Edwards arrived first. He gave the kids money for their banks.

"Thank you, Grandpa," said all the kids.

Then Grandpa Edwards worked in the kitchen making his special dish: Jamaican jerk chicken. Allie handed him the spices he needed. She also helped him mush them into the meat.

Grandma and Grandpa Read arrived next. They brought tomatoes, peppers, and carrots from Grandpa Read's garden and a toy they got at a garage sale.

Aunt Karen, Uncle Bill, and their two girls brought a big fruit salad.

"Wow!" said Allie.

"I can't wait to eat that!"

More people were coming.

"Aunt Leta!" shouted Jonathan.

Leta's family had brought Jamaican rice and peas, flowers, and some bubbles for the kids.

Uncle Fuzz and Aunt Jean's family came with a soccer ball and homemade bread.

People were inside and outside now. They were talking, playing, having fun.

Allie told her cousin, "I made the dessert for today!"

"I can't wait to try it," said Katie.

Allie's mother filled
balloons with water.
Everyone yelled as they
tossed them back and
forth.

"Watch out!"

"Got it!"

"Oh, no!"

After the water balloons, some people husked corn. Uncle Fuzz put his corn husk on his head.

"It's a corn hat!" he said.

Jonathan and some of his cousins put on corn hats, too.

The kids kept playing while the grownups started getting all the food together.

Allie's father started the barbecue grill. He was in charge of the hot dogs and hamburgers. Grandpa Edwards cooked the jerk chicken. Grandpa Read grilled the Slovak sausage.

Finally, everything was ready. Aunt Leta said a prayer. She gave thanks for all the food and for everyone being together.

Allie was happy it was time to eat at last. She was so hungry!

She ate a lot—so did everyone. In fact, soon everyone was saying how full they were. She heard Uncle Bill say, "Great food, but I'm not eating one more thing, no matter how good it is."

What about Allie's peanut-butter treats?

It wasn't fair! Everyone else had given their things to the family. Her present was last, and now nobody would really care since they were all so full.

"Allie, dear, what's the matter?" asked Grandma Read.

She sat down with Allie and listened. Then Grandma said, "Oh, people always say they're too full. Don't worry."

Allie brought out the big platter of peanut-butter treats. Grandmother Read tried to get everyone's attention. "Everyone, please," Grandma said, for the third time.

Allie stood small and alone with the heavy platter. It was quiet suddenly, and they were all looking at her. Her toes felt prickly.

"Allie's the youngest person who made food for us today," Grandma Read said. "You'd better have room left to try these!"

Hands crowded Allie's plate. Everyone said thanks. They all told her what a good job she'd done.

Allie had to try a few treats herself, too.

Then Allie passed the plate around inside.

"Hey," said her cousin Emily, "I want to give everybody these, too."

"Maybe next time," said Aunt Karen. "Or you might do something else. Everyone can do different things."

When Allie came to her parents, her dad said, "Thank you, pumpkin."

"Good work," said her mother. "But I'd like one more thing from my big girl."

"What?" asked Allie.

"Yes," said her dad. "My favorite present, too."

"*What?*" asked Allie—but then she knew what it would be.

A hug!

Here are some things you might want to know more about after reading *For My Family, Love, Allie.*

Recipe for Peanut-Butter Treats

2 cups peanut butter

1 cup powdered milk

1 cup confectioner's sugar

1 cup raisins or chocolate chips

Mix everything together. Shape into small balls.

Leave them plain or roll in coconut flakes, cocoa powder, colored sprinkles, cinnamon and sugar, or mini chocolate chips.

You can refrigerate the treats if they start to get too squishy, or add a little more powdered milk.

Are there people in your family you want to give something to? Here are some ideas:

Make some food.

Lend a favorite book or music tape.

Make a picture for someone's refrigerator.

Are there toys or clothes you've outgrown that you can ask a parent to pass on to someone else in your family?

Is it the time of year when there are flowers or things in your garden you can give?

Write a poem for someone.

Write a letter telling someone why he or she is special to you.

Make a handprint with paint on paper; date it, and add your name and maybe a few special words.

Hugs are good, too!

Library of Congress Cataloging-in-Publication Data

Senisi, Ellen B.

For my family, love, Allie / Ellen B. Senisi

p. cm.

Summary: Allie, whose father is black and mother is white,

decides to make special food as a present for her relatives

when they come for a big family party.

ISBN 0-8075-2539-1

[1. Food—Fiction. 2. Parties—Fiction. 3. Racially mixed people—Fiction.]

I. Title.   PZ7.S4726Fo 1998   [E]—dc21   98-13399

CIP   AC

Text and photographs copyright © 1998 by Ellen B. Senisi.

Published in 1998 by Albert Whitman & Company,

6340 Oakton Street, Morton Grove, Illinois 60053-2723.

Published simultaneously in Canada by General Publishing, Limited, Toronto.

10 9 8 7 6 5 4 3 2 1

The photograph of Katie and Allie at the bottom
of page 19 was taken by Kate Senisi.